Emma Thomson
felicity

# Wand Wishes

## and other stories

By Helen Bailey and Emma Thomson

Illustrated by Emma Thomson

# How to make your felicity Wishes.

## W I S H

With this book comes an extra special wish for you and your best friend.

Hold the book together at each end and both close your eyes.

Wriggle your noses and think of a number under ten.

Open your eyes, whisper the numbers you thought of to each other.

Add these numbers together. This is your

6 ✻ ✻ Magic Number ✻ ✻ 7

13
you

13
best
friend

Place your little finger on the stars, and say your magic number out loud together. Now make your wish quietly to yourselves. And maybe, one day, your wish might just come true.    Love

felicity

x

For Ross, Emma P, Nyree,
and everyone who is someone's best friend.
E.V.T


For Angie Pearson – Happy Days!
H.E.B

FELICITY WISHES © 2002 Emma Thomson
Licensed by White Lion Publishing.

Wand Wishes and Other Stories text © 2002 Helen Bailey and Emma Thomson
Illustrations copyright © 2002 Emma Thomson

First published in Great Britain in 2002 for WHSmith,
Greenbridge Road, Swindon, SN3 3LD
by Hodder Children's Books

The rights of Emma Thomson and Helen Bailey to be identified as the authors
and Emma Thomson as the illustrator of this work have been asserted by them
in accordance with the Copyright, Designs and Patents Act 1988.

10 9 8 7 6 5 4 3 2

A Catalogue record for this book is available from the British Library

ISBN 0 340 85588 6

Printed and bound in Great Britain by Bookmarque Ltd, Croydon, Surrey.

# CONTENTS

Wand Wishes
page 7

* * ✶ * *

Brilliant Blossoms
page 31

* * ✶ * *

Sporting Stars
page 53

* * ✶ * *

# Wand Wishes

The bell for first break rang. Felicity Wishes and her best friends, Polly, Holly and Daisy, flew as fast as they could to get to the sunniest spot on the playing field before anyone else.

They were half-way there, when Felicity remembered she'd left her wand behind.

"You go on without me," she said to her friends. "Save me a spot by the tree – I'll only be a minute."

So the others went on, and Felicity flew back to the Chemistry class where they'd been only minutes before.

The Chemistry teacher, Miss Crystal, was tidying the room, ready for the next lesson. She looked up as Felicity knocked on the door.

"Come in," she said. "What can I do for you, Felicity?"

"Please, Miss Crystal, I think I left my wand here."

"Well," said Miss Crystal thoughtfully. "I haven't *seen* one. Where were you sitting?"

"Just here," said Felicity, walking over to the end of a wooden bench at the front of the room.

"Hmm," said Miss Crystal. "I've already tidied up that area and there was nothing there. Are you sure you left it in here?"

"*Almost* sure," said Felicity, getting down on her hands and knees and looking under the bench. Her tummy was grumbling for her mid-morning Twinkle Bar and she couldn't wait to get out into the sunshine with her friends.

"I suppose I *could* have left it in the hall after assembly," said Felicity, dusting down her stripy tights.

"Well, if it turns up here, I'll let you know. But really, Felicity, you ought to know where your wand is at all times. It might not seem so important now, but when you leave the School of Nine Wishes to become a proper fairy, you'll see how necessary it is to have your wand with you always. It's far better that you get into the habit early on. Now, run along."

Felicity sighed, and looked up at the clock. By the time she'd gone to the school hall to look for her wand,

break would be
nearly over.

"Hmm. Twinkle Bar
or wand-searching?"
she asked herself. It was
a tough decision.

Her tummy grumbled.

"Twinkle Bar it is, then!" she said,
and flew off to join her friends.

"Any luck?" said Polly.

"No, I must have left it in the hall,"
replied Felicity, happily munching
away on her chocolate bar. "I'll go to
lost property after school and see if
anyone's handed it in."

"You can't go a whole day without
your wand!" cried Holly in disbelief.
"You're a fairy!"

"It'll be all right," she said. "I'm
sure we won't have to practice
granting wishes today."

✷ ✷ ✷

But it *wasn't* all right. In geography,

when Felicity was asked to stand at the front of the class and point out all the countries on the globe that began with the letter A, she had nothing to point with. In music class, when it was her turn to conduct the recorders, she had to do it with her finger, and everyone ended up playing at different times – and in art class she couldn't believe it when they were asked to trace round their wands to make a picture. Polly lent her hers.

By the time the last lesson was over, Felicity was desperate for her wand. She'd never realised how much she needed it. Wands weren't just for making wishes, they were handy for all *sorts* of other things.

\* \* \*

11

"Have you had any wands handed in?" Felicity asked the Lost Property Fairy, Miss Sing.

"Sorry, dear, no. In fact, in all my years as a Lost Property Fairy, I've *never* had a wand handed in!"

"Oh," said Felicity quietly, looking down at her toes.

"It's not the sort of thing a fairy normally loses," explained Miss Sing.

"I know," said Felicity, beginning to feel rather sad. "I don't think I'll *ever* make a proper fairy."

Miss Sing tutted. "We'll have no talk like that, Felicity! One day you'll make a *wonderful* fairy. But not without a wand. Why don't you go to the new wand shop, Wand Magic? If you have a really special wand, you'll *always* want to know where it is."

Feeling instantly perkier, Felicity flew off in the direction of the shops. Shopping, it has to be said, was one of Felicity's favourite things.

✳ ✳ ✳

Wand Magic in Little Blossoming had only been open for a few days, but already it was said to be the best fairy wand shop for miles. Even before you reached it, you could see the pavement outside glittering. Each hand-made wand was displayed in a glass case, on a deep pink, velvet cushion with gold trimming.

Felicity stood in the doorway, her mouth wide open in wonder.

"Can I help?" asked the friendly assistant.

"I'd like a new wand, please," said

Felicity. Then she noticed something. "You've got glitter on your nose!"

"I know, it's working with wands. It gets everywhere! Now, what sort of wand would you like? You look to me like a novice fairy, so I imagine you'll need a Standard Swing. Do you have a handle colour you'd especially like?"

"I was rather hoping for a more special sort of wand – something that I would want to look after properly," said Felicity, who had just spotted some more glitter on the assistant's ear.

"Well," said the assistant, smiling broadly and clapping her hands, "today is your lucky day! Let me just show you this…" and she reached under the counter and took out a small golden key. "Come with me."

Felicity and the assistant left the main shop.

"I wouldn't normally take customers into the stock room, you understand," the assistant said, putting the key into the lock, "but we've just had a delivery of... THESE!"

She threw open the door to reveal a room bathed in the most twinkly silver light Felicity had ever seen. Dozens of beautiful silver starred wands lined the shelves.

Felicity gasped. "They're beautiful!"

"Breathtaking, aren't they? And silver stars – who'd have thought! Gold is such a classic, but these really *are* what you'd call 'more special', I think. And I guarantee you'll be the only fairy in Little Blossoming with a silver starred wand, which really *is* special!"

\* \* \*

Felicity literally danced out of the wand shop – and she danced all the way home too, waving her silver starred wand as she went. Fairies she

passed stopped and stared, some
even smiling and waving when they
saw her unusual wand.

"This is what it must feel like to be
famous," she thought. "I can't wait to
show everyone at school tomorrow!"

That night Felicity slept with her
wand under her pillow. In
the morning she carefully
made a little tag for it.

There wasn't a fairy at the School
of Nine Wishes who hadn't heard
about Felicity's wand by the time she
arrived. Excited groups of giggling
fairies kept anxiously turning around
in assembly trying to catch a glimpse
of her spectacular silver wand.

"It's beautiful," sighed Polly. "My
gold wand looks so dowdy in
comparison."

"It's just too sparkly for words,"
said Daisy, putting a hand over
her eyes.

"It's stunning," said Holly reluctantly. Holly always prided herself on being, if not the trendiest fairy, then certainly the one who always got noticed out of the four friends. Felicity had beaten her to it this time.

"Well, you can all have one too," said Felicity. "They had lots in the shop – the delivery had only just arrived. Go on, why don't we *all* get them, then we can match!"

"Yes!" said Polly, excitedly.

"Let's!!" agreed Daisy.

"We can put our old wands away for a rainy day!" said Holly, suddenly cheering up.

\* \* \*

All day Felicity was bombarded with questions by fairies wanting to know about her new silver starred wand.

"How heavy is it?" "Is it easy to wave?" "How did you find it?" "Does its sparkliness get in the way of you seeing things properly?" "Do you know that you've got glitter on your nose?"

Finally the bell sounded for the end of the last lesson, and Polly, Holly, Felicity and Daisy flew straight to Wand Magic. Only, when they turned the corner on to Star Street, they couldn't believe what they saw.

A queue of fairies stretched from the wand shop, past Sugar Twist, the newsagents, past Fresh and Bright, the dry cleaners, past the Post Office, past Ice-Cream Dreams, and finally ended at Sparkles, the café on the corner.

"Goodness," said Polly. "It looks like we're not the only ones who thought about getting a new wand!"

"I don't know if I can queue for all this time, even for something as beautiful as a silver wand like Felicity's," said Daisy, anxiously.

"But I really want one," pleaded Polly.

"And if we *don't* get one, we'll be the only fairies in school without one!" said Holly.

"Well, I don't need to queue," said Felicity, wiggling her wand casually and making them all shield their eyes for a moment. "So I can keep

you supplied with take-away hot chocolates to keep your strength up while you wait!"

When they finally reached the front of the queue for *Wand Magic*, all three fairies had drunk enough hot chocolate to last them for ever.

It was worth it, though, when they found out that they had got the last three sparkly silver starred wands in the shop.

\* \* \*

The next day, the School of Nine Wishes was surrounded by a glittery silver glow that shone for miles. There wasn't a fairy in the school without glitter on her nose. Even Fairy Godmother had a wand that boasted one of the new sparkly silver stars.

"Good morning, fairies," welcomed Fairy Godmother. "Before we begin assembly today, I'd like to introduce you all to a new pupil."

A timid-looking fairy shuffled on to the stage. "This is Tilly, who has just moved to Little Blossoming. I hope you will all do your best to make her feel one of the family at the School of Nine Wishes."

Tilly wasn't in any of Felicity's classes, which Felicity found a little disappointing. She liked to be as friendly as she could, even to people she didn't know, and she had been secretly looking forward to taking the new fairy under her wing.

✳ ✳ ✳

It wasn't until lunch-time that Felicity saw Tilly again, quietly sitting alone in the dining hall with her packed lunch.

"Hello there," said Felicity, sitting

down next to her. "I'm Felicity –
Felicity Wishes. I saw you in
assembly this morning,
you're Tilly,
aren't you?"

"Yes," said Tilly timidly.
"Would you like to come and eat
your lunch with me and my friends?
They're ever so nice, I'm sure you'll
like them."
Tilly looked up at Felicity, then
down at her lunch. She shook her
head.

"No… no… no, it's ok," she said, looking awkward.

"Oh, please do! I love making new friends," said Felicity.

"Really, no, I'm afraid I…" and Tilly's eyes welled up with tears. "I'm afraid I'd only embarrass you."

"Tilly!" said Felicity. "What *do* you mean?" and she put her arm round the new fairy's shoulder.

"I- I- I just don't fit in," said Tilly, her voice wobbling with emotion.

"Of course you do," said Felicity comfortingly. "You're a fairy, and that's all you need to be to fit in here."

A large tear rolled down Tilly's face and plopped on to the table.

"No," said Tilly, taking a deep breath. "You don't understand. I really *don't* fit in…"

Tilly rummaged around in her school bag, finally pulling out a

wand with a big golden star on the
end of it. "Look! It's not silver!" she
said, wiping the tear from the table.
"Everyone else has silver stars. I'm the
only one with a gold one. I'll *never*
fit in!" and she buried her head in
her hands and sobbed.

Felicity looked down at Tilly's gold
starred wand, then at her own
beautiful silver starred wand. She
put on her thoughtful look. It was
true, everyone else *did* have silver
stars. She couldn't get another one
from the shop for Tilly because Holly,

Polly and Daisy had taken the last three. There was only one thing to do.

"The only reason I have a silver starred wand is because I lost my gold one," said Felicity. "I was ever so upset when I lost it. Why don't we swap? Gold is more my sort of colour any way – it goes with my hair. Really," she continued, "you'd be doing me a favour. These silver stars have a habit of spreading their glitter everywhere and I'm fed up of brushing it off my nose all the time!"

Tilly took her hands away from her face and looked up. "Really?" she said quietly.

"Really," said Felicity, carefully peeling off her name tag and handing over her wand. "Now, why don't we go and find Holly, Polly and Daisy to have some lunch – I'm starving!"

And, waving their new wands, they flew off to join the others.

it takes a very
special sort of friend

to give away something
they truly treasure

# Brilliant Blossoms

It was a beautiful spring day in Little Blossoming. As Felicity Wishes flew through the sparkling golden gates of the School of Nine Wishes, birds were singing, flowers were bursting into bloom and the blue sky was dotted with little clouds so perfect they could have been made out of cotton-wool.

"What a shame to have to go to school on a day like this!" she thought.

Fairy Godmother obviously had the same idea, as she announced that they would all go on a nature flight through Nine Wish Wood when assembly was over.

All the fairies were given a list of plants and flowers to look for on the flight and, excitedly, they set of in groups of four, flying through the wood, weaving in and out of the trees. Daisy flew ahead looking eagerly for the plants on the list: Snowdrop, Crocus, Primrose, Bluebell, Daffodil. Polly, Felicity and Holly followed her, nattering away. Suddenly there was a shout.

"Ow!"

"What's the matter?" asked Daisy, turning to see all three of her friends sitting on the woodland floor rubbing their heads.

"We were too busy chatting and not looking where we were flying," said Felicity, picking leaves out of her crown. "We flew into a tree!"

"We've been flying for hours!"
moaned Holly, exaggerating as
usual. "My wings are aching. How
many flowers have you seen, Daisy?"

"None," said Daisy, looking down
at the list.

"Not one?" asked Polly, raising her
eyebrows.

"Not even a single petal," sighed
Daisy, checking her list again.

The fairies looked around Nine

Wish Wood. It was bare. Even in the little sunlit spots between the trees, there were no flowers.

Just then, Daisy noticed a single, tiny, purple crocus. She knelt down and whispered, "Hello, little crocus. Are you lonely here on your own?" Even though Daisy knew it was just the breeze of the other fairies flying past, the tiny flower seemed to nod back at her. "Don't worry," she said. "I'll think of something!"

✳ ✳ ✳

None of the fairies had managed to find any of the things on the list, though plenty of them now had dirty shoes, muddy hands and holes in their tights. Still, it was much more fun than sitting in a classroom all morning.

Daisy had spent the whole day since they got back to school thinking

about the lonely crocus in the wood –
and now she had a plan.

At the last bell of the school day,
as all the fairies streamed out of the
school gates giggling and laughing,
Daisy stayed behind.

With quivering wings she made
her way to Fairy Godmother's office.
The door was slightly open and Daisy
peeped round the corner. The room
was very large and the walls were
lined with antique wands and shelves
bursting with huge books, with titles
such as *The Story of the Modern Wish*
and *The Art of Caring for Your Wings*.

Fairy Godmother was resting in a
large golden chair with her feet on
the desk, flicking through a pile of
holiday brochures. She was planning
a visit to Fairy World. 'A Week of
Carefree Magic' boasted the front of
the brochure.

When Fairy Godmother still didn't

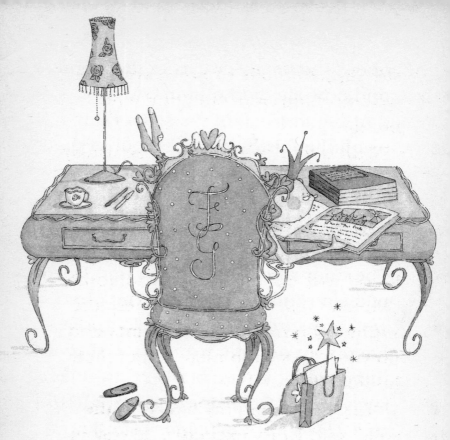

notice her, Daisy gave a little cough.
Fairy Godmother looked up so
sharply and tried to take her legs off
the desk so quickly, her chair tipped
backwards and her crown fell off her
head. Straightening her crown and
reaching for her shoes, she asked
Daisy to come in. Daisy noticed that

she slipped a pile of homework she was marking over the Fairy World brochure.

With a face as red as a rose, Daisy told Fairy Godmother about the lonely, purple crocus.

"I have to admit, I hadn't realised just what a poor state Nine Wish Wood was in," said Fairy Godmother. "None of last year's fairies were the slightest bit interested in plants and flowers. They didn't like to get their hands dirty."

"I LOVE getting my hands in the soil," said Daisy excitedly. "Blossom Fairies don't worry about clean hands!"

"So you'd like to be a Blossom Fairy when you leave school?" Fairy Godmother said, smiling kindly at the embarrassed young fairy in front of her.

"More than *anything*," said Daisy.

"Could I plant some flowers in the wood? I'd make sure they were the sort of flowers which should grow in a Fairy Wood."

Fairy Godmother was very tired. It had been a long day and she just wanted to go home, have a long, hot bubble bath and plan her holiday.

"As long as you promise to tell someone when you are going into the wood and don't disturb the soil too much," she told a delighted Daisy.

\* \* \*

When Daisy got home, she reached under her bed and pulled out a pile of *Glorious Fairy Gardens* and *Magical Garden Makeovers* magazines. These were her favourite types of magazine and she spent hours reading them. When the other fairies had started to tease her gently about "starting to look like a flower" if she read them any more, she began tucking them inside copies of *Fairy Girl*.

In the back of one of the copies of *Magical Garden Makeovers*, in amongst the advertisements for magic beans, green finger hand cream and gardening wands with rosewood stems, she found the advertisement she had been looking for.

Woodland Wonders
Create the perfect display of wonderful
Woodland Wonders flowers in no time at all.
Suppliers of Magical Bulbs
and Seeds to fairies worldwide.
Just sprinkle with morning dew and
success is GUARANTEED!

It was perfect!

\* \* \*

The wooden box filled with magical bulbs and seeds arrived a few days  later. There were golden seeds so tiny you could mistake them for sparkle dust; larger oval-shaped seeds that seemed to change colour the longer you held them in your hand; bulbs which looked like fat paper pebbles, and one that looked like one of the fairy cakes that Felicity had burnt in cookery class last term.

Taking the seeds to her greenhouse, Daisy carefully filled some seed trays with earth, made tiny holes with the end of her wand and, in each hole, planted a different seed. She gently brushed the earth over the top, before patting it down with the star on the end of her wand. Almost as soon as she began to water the trays with

distilled morning dew, tiny green
shoots began to appear, just as the
advert had promised.

"Magic!" said Daisy, out loud to
herself.

\* \* \*

The moment she woke up the next
morning, Daisy rushed out of bed
and ran down to the greenhouse to
see how her seedlings were getting
on. She didn't even get dressed.

"Good morning!" she said to them,
as she filled up her watering can.

"How are you today?" she asked,
as she inspected their leaves.

\* \* \*

For the next week, Daisy spent
every spare moment she had in the
greenhouse with her Woodland
Wonders, watering, whispering and
occasionally singing words of
encouragement to the growing
green shoots, which were getting

bigger every day. Some
of them had now got
so big that Daisy was
able to plant them
out in proper
pots.

One morning, while Daisy was
deep in conversation with one of the
smallest flowers, Felicity popped her
head round the greenhouse door.

"Hello! We're all off to Polly's for tea
and cake," she said. "We wondered if
you wanted to come – we've hardly
seen you lately – but it sounds as if
you've got someone with you."

Daisy giggled.

"That was me talking to my flowers
to help them grow strong enough for
when I..." Daisy stopped. She had
decided that the magical Woodland

Wonders would be a surprise, not only for the lonely, purple crocus but for her friends as well. "…For when I leave them to come and have a large slice of cake at Polly's!"

As Daisy went into the house to wash her hands, Felicity smiled and raised her eyes to the sky.

"Blossom Fairies," she said, shaking her head. "They're all the same."

✳ ✳ ✳

The day had come for Daisy to plant the woodland garden.

She had planned to take the plant pots to the wood, but they were too heavy and she would have to make several trips. So, instead, she carefully dug around the plants with her special silver trowel and, being careful not to disturb the roots, put them into a basket.

As she left the greenhouse she felt a bit sad. It seemed very bare. Just rows and rows of pots with only their labels to show there had ever been anything there. She would miss looking after them. Still, the woodland garden would look fabulous.

So she set off to Nine Wish Wood to begin a happy afternoon of planting.

\* \* \*

Having had no success trying the doorbell, Felicity and Polly looked round the back of Daisy's house. Daisy had been so busy in her garden recently, they had decided to surprise her and take her to Sparkles for a hot chocolate.

"The greenhouse door is open," said Polly. "She's probably in there having a good natter to her plants."

"That's strange. Daisy usually has the door closed to keep it warm," said Felicity, becoming worried.

But when they arrived at the greenhouse door, all they saw were empty plant pots and soil covering the floor.

"Oh no!" shrieked Felicity. "Look at Daisy's greenhouse. It's ruined! Someone has taken all Daisy's plants!"

"Who in Little Blossoming would do

a thing like that?" said Polly.

Felicity looked at some of the plant labels. Yellow Sparkle Primrose, Sunshine Daffodil, Musical Bluebells, Spotted Orchid.

"We can't let Daisy see this, she'll be heartbroken," she said. "You know how important Daisy's plants are to her."

"What are we going to do?" Polly asked Felicity.

"Look, these are the plant labels, let's see if we can replace the plants before Daisy notices."

So Polly and Felicity flew quickly to the Roots 'N' Shoots garden centre. After explaining to the assistant why they were in such a rush, the assistant left her half-eaten sandwich and copy of *Fairy Girl* on the counter and went to help them match up plants with the labels Felicity had taken from the pots. In no time at all they had the plants they were looking for.

* * *

It took the fairies three flights between the garden centre and Daisy's house to transfer all the plants. There was no time to waste!

Eventually they finished. The greenhouse was full of plants once more.

Felicity and Polly left Daisy a note to meet them in Sparkles. After all that work, they needed a hot chocolate more than anything!

Just as they were scraping the last little bits of cream from the bottom of their glasses, Daisy flew in with a smile as sparkly as a star.

"Thank goodness you two are still here!" she said, sitting down with a thump. "I need a double creamy chocolate shake right now! I've had such a surprise!"

And Daisy began to tell her fairy friends the whole story: about the conversation with Fairy Godmother, about the advert, the magic seeds and how sad she had been to see them go,

and finally how happy the purple crocus had looked when she had surrounded it with a woodland garden.

"But that's not all!" said Daisy, her eyes as wide as saucers. "I got home just now to find that those magic seeds really *are* magic. All the pots that were empty are now full again! I was telling the flowers on the way to the forest how much I would miss them, and now I can see them every day at home!"

Felicity nudged Polly and Polly winked at Felicity, but Daisy was too excited to notice them, or their unusually dirty hands...

## Sporting Stars

Fairy Godmother was beginning her announcements for the school week.

"For those of you who have a musical twinkle in your heart, you will be pleased to know that Miss Jingle will be starting a recorder club on Tuesday," said Fairy Godmother. "Meet after school under the large oak tree in the first playing field."

Felicity Wishes was sitting at the back of the assembly hall, casually plaiting Holly's hair until Miss Crystal, the science teacher, gave her a 'you know you shouldn't be doing that' sort of look.

"Flying Club is cancelled on Wednesday lunchtime," continued Fairy Godmother. "As most of you know, Miss Fluttering is still in hospital following her unfortunate accident last week."

The fairies giggled. They had noticed that the flagpole had been mended.

"Finally, young fairies," she announced, "I'm sure you don't need reminding to bring a sports kit with you tomorrow for School Sports Day."

Excited fairy noises rippled around the hall.

Fairy Godmother clapped her hands for silence and the fairies all held their wands in their right hands and recited the Fairy Motto, before flying out of the school hall. They were so excited they could hardly fly straight.

"Sports Day!" said Felicity. "Hearts will win this year. I can feel it in my wings!"

"Nonsense," said Holly, grabbing Polly's hand and raising it triumphantly in the air. "Stars always win!"

There were three houses at the School of Nine Wishes: Hearts, Stars and Flowers. Felicity was in Hearts, Holly and Polly were in Stars and Daisy was in Flowers.

Polly was taking sports day very seriously.

"Stars will definitely win this year," she said. "I've been training with weighted wands. Not only will it come in useful for lifting up those heavy pillows when I become a Tooth Fairy, it means no-one will beat Stars in the tug of war!" Polly pushed up her sleeves and flexed her muscles. The other fairies doubled up in fits of giggles.

"I'd hate to think what your muscles looked like *before* your training!" squealed Holly.

"Don't be so sure that Stars are going to win, Pol," said Felicity. "Now is the time to tell you that I have been secretly practising my Front Flutter Twist every night before I get into bed. In fact," she continued, "it's *how* I get into bed."

The Front Flutter Twist was one of the most difficult wing strokes a fairy could achieve, and the most exciting event at Sports Day. In flying lessons, Miss Fluttering had made the fairies draw endless diagrams, answer hundreds of questions and take two written tests before they were even allowed to attempt it. If you got it wrong, you could sprain your wing so badly you might never fly straight again.

To the gasps of the class, Felicity was what Miss Fluttering called "a natural". What Felicity had never admitted to anyone was that she hadn't meant to attempt it in the first place. Having spent too long in the changing rooms doing her hair, she had dashed on to the playing field late, tripped up into the air, tried to regain her balance and landed, amazingly, on her feet.

\* \* \*

The next day the fairies gathered on the tennis courts, nervously chattering and giggling and crowding round to

look at the list of names and events pinned to the fence. Fairies who weren't huddled round the lists were warming up with some last minute exercises, or frantically calling out for lost plimsolls or a spare wand for relay practice.

Fairy Godmother sounded a large bell for the start of the games.

As neither Felicity nor her friends were due to compete until later, they decided to watch the Single Circuit Freestyle Dash.

Jostling for a front row position near the finishing line, they waited excitedly for Miss Meandering, the geography teacher, to wave her wand for the start of the race.

Holly nudged Felicity and pointed at the fairy in the Star T-Shirt at the start line. It was Amelia, one of the sportiest fairies at the School of Nine Wishes.

"I told you Stars were going to win," she whispered to Felicity, who had noticed with horror that her Housemate, Tilly, was racing against Amelia.

"With Tilly running for Hearts it will be close," said Felicity, not entirely confidently. She wasn't sure that Tilly, who wanted to be a Dream Fairy, would even make it off the starting line, let alone reach the finishing one.

"Who's flying for Flowers?" asked Daisy, craning her neck to see the flyers lining up.

"No-one who can beat Stars!" said Holly.

All eyes were glued to the three nervous fairies waiting to race. A hush settled on the crowd and, in the bright sunshine, Miss Meandering lifted her wand high above her head and said loudly, "Ready...Steady...FLY!" As she brought her wand down with a swoop, the fairies were off.

To everyone's amazement, Tilly was first off the line with the fastest Forward Flapping the girls had ever seen.

Amelia, with an impressive Back Flutter, quickly caught up with her but coming up on the inside lane was the fairy from the Flower team, gliding along as easily as a boat slipping through water.

"STARS!" yelled Polly at the top of her voice.

"HEARTS!" shouted Felicity as loudly as she could.

"AMELIAAAAAAAAAAAAAA!" cried Holly.

"TILLYYYYYYY!" screamed Felicity.

It was close. Hearts and Stars were within a wing tip of each other, with one corner to turn before the final fly to the finishing line. The atmosphere was electric. Fairies shouted encouragement as loudly as they could.

Stars were in the lead as Amelia raced towards the finish, but Tilly, who looked as if she was beginning to run out of wing power, suddenly got another burst of energy and, spurred on by the cries from the crowd, increased the speed of her Forward Flap to bring her within a

whisper of Amelia. Just as it seemed
Tilly might take over, the fairy from
the Flower team put all she had into
her quiet glide and crept over the
finishing line.

Flowers had won.

"Yippeee!" squealed Daisy, clapping her hands.

"It's just one race," Holly reminded her.

Polly went off to get changed for the Tug of War and Holly, Daisy and Felicity stood looking up at the results board that Fairy Godmother was filling in.

"Stars have won the Wing Assisted High Jump!" said Daisy.

"Hearts have won the Flying Leap!" cried Felicity.

Holly couldn't believe her eyes. "Flowers are in the lead – look!"

"It's very close – and it's not over yet!" said Felicity. "Let's go and see Polly's pillow-lifting muscles in action!"

\* \* \*

The fairies lined up eagerly by the side of the spectator section for the Tug of War. Polly spotted her fairy friends in the crowd and waved.

"GO ON, POLLY!" they chorused.

"Oh no!" said Felicity. "Who shall I shout for? Polly is tugging against

Hearts! Do I shout for Polly or do I cheer for Hearts?"

"Call for both!" suggested Daisy. "That way, whoever wins, you can't lose!"

When the wand had been waved and the fairies started to tug, Felicity took it in turns to call for her friend and for her team. "Pollyyy!... Heartssss... Pollyyyyyy... Heartsssss!"

Polly certainly *had* been practising with weighted wands, and it wasn't long before the fairies from Hearts were on the floor. Stars had won!

\* \* \*

The day had been exhausting. Most of the events had taken place by now and fairies with croaky voices and achy legs bounced with the little energy they had left up to the results board. It was even closer than before.

"Hearts are only one point behind Flowers!" shrieked Felicity, as she ran off to get changed.

"Stars are only two points behind!" said Holly.

"Whoever wins the final event will win the whole day for their team!" gasped Polly.

The final event of the day was the Front Flutter Twist. All the fairies from the School of Nine Wishes formed a semi-circle around the soft sand area where the Twist would be performed. Each fairy had only one chance to get it right. The fairy who gained the most height with tight control would win four points. *Everything* rested on this event.

✳ ✳ ✳

Fastening her hair with her lucky slide (the same one she had used on the day she had done the Twist when she tripped in flying class), Felicity took a deep breath. It was her chance to win for her team. She knew she could do it.

She was just about to leave the changing room when she heard a noise. It sounded like sobbing. It was coming from the gym cupboard.

"Hello?" she called out. "Are you alright?"

"Not really," sniffed the little voice.

Felicity peeped round the door, but all she could see were piles of netballs and skipping ropes.

"Why don't you come out and tell me what's the matter?" asked Felicity gently.

But the sniffing fairy refused to come out – or let Felicity come in.

"I'm doing the Front Flutter Twist, y-y-you see."

"Are you nervous?" asked Felicity.

"I'll lose. I *always* lose! Now I'm going to lose it for the entire team!" The sound of sniffing behind the netballs got louder.

"It doesn't matter," said Felicity gently. "Fairy Godmother has always said that it's not about the winning, it's about the taking part and trying your best."

"I know..." said the sobbing voice, "but once, just once, it would be nice not to come last."

"If there is one thing I've learnt at the School of Nine Wishes it's that you have to really believe you can do something," said Felicity encouragingly. "If you believe you can do it, then you will!"

"B-b-b-but I *can't* d-d-do it!" sobbed the fairy.

"Of course you can! Believe you can win. Promise me when you go out there, just before you do your Twist, that you'll close your eyes and say to yourself *I can, I can*, over and over."

"If you really think it will help," said the little voice in the cupboard.

"I'm sure of it. Good luck!" said Felicity, as she turned to leave the changing room.

\* \* \*

Outside, the sun beat down. The three competing fairies stood in front of Fairy Godmother. Felicity looked sideways at the fairy on the Flower team, who was blowing her nose with a spotted hankie.

Fairy Godmother cleared her throat.

"Fairies. As you know, the scores are *very* close. The result of this Twist will determine which house

will win! First prize is the school cup.
Second prize is the school medal, and
the runners-up will all receive a pink
rosette. Could the fairies from each
team take their place?"

A nervous hush descended on the
school. Fairy Godmother raised her

wand. Felicity glanced at the crowd, at her friends, and at the fairy in the Flowers team, who was talking to herself under her breath.

"Ready...Steady...FLUTTER!" cried Fairy Godmother, swooping her wand.

All three fairies bent their knees, straightened their backs and flung themselves forward, fluttering their wings as they twisted.

The crowd gasped as they saw the fairy from the Flowers team twist high above Felicity and the fairy from Stars, then land with perfect precision.

Felicity managed a perfect Front Flutter Twist but didn't gain as much height as the fairy from Flowers, and the fairy from Stars landed in a crumpled heap in the sand.

It was all over in the fluttering of a wing.

Flowers had won!

Fairies ran from all directions on to the sand to give their team members a hug.

"Flowers won!" said Polly. "I don't believe it! I was so sure that Felicity would win this event!"

"How strange," said Daisy. "I wonder why she didn't get as high as she usually does?"

Holly went over and patted Felicity's back. "I'm sorry you lost," she said.

Just then a crowd of fairies from the Flowers team flew past, carrying the fairy from the gym cupboard high above their heads. She was smiling the biggest smile Felicity had ever seen.

Felicity waved and smiled.

"What do you mean, lost?" said Felicity, linking arms with her friends. "I've won a wonderful pink

rosette that will match my stripy
tights perfectly. Now, how about
an ice-cream to finish the day off
properly?"

Collect all four Felicity Wishes story collections:

* * *

Fashion Fiasco

Dancing Dreams

Spooky Sleepover

Wand Wishes

*